MW00915922

Fluffy Bunny
MAKES NEW FRIENDS

WRITTEN BY
KELLY KLINE

ILLUSTRATED BY
AMBER LEIGH LUECKE

Interior design by Amber Leigh Luecke
www.amberleighluecke.com

ISBN: 978-1-0879-9235-8 (hardcover)
ISBN: 978-1-0879-9239-6 (ebook)

Printed in the United States

DEDICATION

This book is dedicated to my grandchildren,

Jocelyn, E.J., and Anthony....
you are my inspiration.

Remember that you're never too old to change your
goals and dream new dreams....just be sure you follow
them; to my daughter, Cecelia, and son-in-law, Eric,
for giving me my grandchildren; and to Aldo for your
encouragement, believing in me,
and being my other half through this
crazy journey that is our life.

I love you all!

Today was Fluffy Bunny's first day of school and he had butterflies in his tummy. He was scared that no one would be his friend. He was different from the other kids because he was so fluffy. He thought the other kids would make fun of him like his brothers and sisters did.

When he walked in the classroom, he saw a little skunk sitting all alone in the corner. He decided to go say hi.

"Hello," he said. "My name is Fluffy Bunny. What's your name?"
The little skunk answered, "My name is Samantha Skunk."
Fluffy asked, "Do you want to be friends?"
"Yes. The other kids don't want to be my friend," said Samantha.
"Why not?" asked Fluffy.

"I'm different from the other kids. Sometimes I smell funny," said Samantha with her head down.
"Well, I'll be your friend. Let's sit together," said Fluffy.

And they did!

At recess, Fluffy and Samantha went out to play.
They saw a little turtle all by himself so they
decided to go talk to him.

"Hello. My name is Fluffy Bunny and this is Samantha Skunk. What's your name?"

The turtle answered...very...very...slowly, "H-h-hello...my name is Timmy...Turtle."

Fluffy asked, "Do you want to be friends?"

"Y-y-yes...I don't have...many friends," said Timmy.

"Why not?" asked Fluffy.

"I–I–I'm...different...from the other kids. I'm...too...slow...so I can't run fast...and play like them," said Timmy Turtle sadly.

"Well, we'll be your friends," said Fluffy.

"Yes. Let's go play!" said Samantha.

Then Fluffy saw a little squirrel sitting in a tree watching the other kids play. "Hey, Samantha and Timmy. Look at that squirrel all by herself in the tree.

Let's go see if she wants to play," said Fluffy.
"Okay!" said Samantha and Timmy.

"Hello. My name is Fluffy, this is Samantha, and this is Timmy. What's your name?"

The little squirrel answered quietly, "Hi. My name is Skyler Squirrel."

Fluffy Bunny asked, "Do you want to be our friend?"

Skyler said, "I'd like that. I don't make friends easily."

"Why not?" asked Fluffy.

"I'm different from the other kids. I'm shy and I don't always know what to say."

"That's okay. We'll be your friends," said Fluffy Bunny.

"Yes!" said Samantha and Timmy. "Let's go play!"

And they did!

Some of the other kids made fun of them because Fluffy Bunny was so fluffy and Samantha Skunk was smelly and Timmy Turtle was slow and Skyler Squirrel was shy.

But for the rest of the day, the four friends sat
together and played together whenever they could.

They were sad when they had to go home, but they knew they would see each other the next day. Fluffy Bunny told his new friends, "Just because we're different doesn't mean we can't be friends."

They decided from that day forward they would
be lifelong friends.

CPSIA information can be obtained
at www.ICGtesting.com
Printed in the USA
BVHW090006011221
622866BV00004B/149

9 781087 992358